ANYTHING

ALSO BY IAN WILD

PLAYS
Homage to an American in Paris
Spaghetti Western
Marco Polo's Toilet Brush
The Milk of Human Kindness
Somebody and Nobody
The Pirates in Short Pants
Mrs Shakespeare
Rachmaninov's Maid

POETRY
Intercourse With Cacti
Holy Cow

NOVELS
The Naked Umbrella Thieves
The Celtic Tyger Hunt
My Fourth Dimensional Friend

PROSE
The Woman Who Swallowed the Book of Kells
(Short Stories)
Growing Up Engaged (Essays)

Ian Wild

Anything Strange

ISBN 978-1723075872

All writing and illustrations by Ian Wild

Many thanks to Conor Power and
The Southern Star for first publishing this work.
Thanks also to Perry O'Donovan for his encouragement.
Credit also to Louis, Perry and Mrs Wild where it's due.
Mr. James Harpur is also thanked for casting his benevolent
eye over the following words and improving how they sit.

CONTENTS

Introduction	7
1. Irish Elastic Airways	10
2. Whalesong	14
3. A Good Word for the Rain	18
4. Bah! Noddy Holder	23
5. Leaning Tower of Ballydehob	28
6. Gearoid Hill	33
7. Lazy Salmon	38
8. The Trouble with Machines	43
9. The Secret Life of Biros	48
10. Hearing Aid	53
11. Trans-Ireland Moustache	57
12. A Day at the Races	62
13. The Funniest Man on Earth	67
14. Genetically Modified Cars	72
15. There's Nothing Stranger Than...	77
16. Leonardo – Undiscovered Sketch	82
17. Identity Theft	86
18. Russian Weather Machine	91
19. Halloween Special	96
20. We have the Technology	101

INTRODUCTION

Between 2008 and 2012, I wrote a monthly column for the *Southern Star* magazine *Starlife* and later intermittently, for the paper itself. The magazine, under the editorship of Conor Power was an eclectic mix of features and interviews and I was afforded by Conor – brave man – a seemingly unlimited latitude in my scribblings. In fact, I'd had the idea of writing a column called *Anything Strange* for some time. For those of you who are unfamiliar with the politesse and social mores of West Cork, "Anything strange?" is a secondary utterance in a greeting between friends along the lines of "What's new?" One might meet a friend or acquaintance in Clonakilty or Enniskeane and open a conversational passing of the time of day thus:

"Hi Meehawl."[1]

"Hello Ian. The weather's coming in nasty from the west."

"Yes. Those clouds look very black."

"Anything strange?"

---

[1] Spelling courtesy of James Stephens.

At which point I would recount perhaps some small high or lowlight of recent passing, which would not be in the least bit strange.

"My cat's run away. The brown one."

Or:

"Couldn't get my fecking car to start this morning."

I've sometimes, in my more courageous moments, attempted to use the conversational gambit myself. Sadly, I've never had a local tell me anything mind-bendingly strange on enquiry. Though I'd longingly hope for a reply along the lines of:

"Anything strange Mehawl?"

"Well, now, since you ask, my brother, yesterday, ate a cauliflower that he'd found down at the bottom of the garden. And an hour after eating it, didn't he go out to the river and begin throwing his shoes into the water, to see would they float all the way down to the bridge in Kinsale. Eight pairs he threw in. And you know, only two shoes managed the whole trip. But come here, Ian boy, the very strangest thing about the whole situation was that the two shoes that drifted through Bandon and Innishannon and out towards the sea, well – *they didn't match!* One was brown, and the other was black! What do you make of that?"

No, no fascinating recent events of Daliesque strangeness were ever recollected for my eager ears on sallying forth with this wonderfully eccentric greeting. Disappointing. Very. So my column allowed me to compensate for this little bit of conversational anti-climax in my life. Setting myself up, notionally, as a roving reporter around the County, I went searching for strangeness in West Cork knowing (as we all do) that it couldn't be far away. In fact, I didn't have to look particularly hard at all. I soon found it was constantly there, sitting in the same room, working at a computer. Never further away than my own self.

IRISH ELASTIC AIRWAYS

As a new columnist for the *Star,* I've been asked to get out and about and focus on anything that's a little bit out of the ordinary around the county. Now it happens I had to go up to Dublin recently and chose a cheap flight with Irish Elastic Airways. With oil prices fluctuating and the globe hotting up, public transport faces ever-increasing challenges to get us from A to B cheaply and in a way that won't leave polar bears selling the Big Issue on street corners. So news that people are commuting from Cork to Dublin and back by giant catapult, comes as no surprise. The man behind Irish Elastic Airways, Bernard Kerr, met me on the docks in Cork. I have to say, I'm obviously not the only one to get butterflies about flying. Behind a vast iron Y bolted to the quayside, a line of prospective catapultees were laughing nervously as they watched a man clamber into a pouch. As the elastic was winched back, I asked Bernard about his enterprise.

"Hang on, there's one just taking off........"

There was a colossal twang, then a whoosh.

"Arrrrrrgghghgghggh!!!!!"

Once the man had vanished like a missile over Cork City, Bernard turned back to me:

"Yes?"

"Bernard," I asked, "Is shooting people from one side of the country to the other by giant catapult really the answer to our transport problems?"

"Well it's fast. Dublin to Cork takes twenty-five minutes. It's cheap. The elastic only needs changing after every ten thousand flights. We can send people for five euros return, and there are family flights, up to six all in the one pouch. If you don't mind getting a bit wet at the other end, it certainly beats the traffic jams. Basically people are fired off in lifejackets and land in the sea at the other side of the country. It's perfectly safe, as there's no sharks off our coastline. Catapultees from Cork land in the Irish Sea and face a ten-minute swim into Dublin."

Watching a young couple clamber into the large pouch together, I asked Bernard about the safety of the system and talk of fatalities.

"It *is* safe," he assured me. "We tested the system by firing mice in lifejackets, then dogs and chimpanzees before moving on to humans. Last month a circus was late for an engagement in Galway and we fired five elephants over. That made a bit of a splash in more ways than one. You get fatalities on the road. And with us you'll never crash at the top of a mountain and have to eat your crew, which happened with one airline. You have to accept that if you step out of your front door you could be run over. Hang on, there's another........."

There was a double scream as the catapult twanged again. Bernard continued:

"We've had a few people fall short of the Irish Sea, it's true. But they weren't holding their arms out properly. You see, you have to stay streamlined, make yourself aerodynamic or over several hundred miles you'll create wind resistance and fall short of the target. We *did* have to change the colour of our lifejackets from red and blue, because people by the sea were complaining of a plague of Supermen. But though we've had a couple of pavement pancakes, a few collisions and fatalities from people trying to scramble round in mid-air and turn back, we think Irish Elastic Airways are flying in the right direction for the years ahead.

"Any plans for the future." I asked as I clambered up into the hot seat.

"Oh definitely." Bernard assured me, "Once we've got stronger elastic sorted from our suppliers we'll be starting transatlantic flights – people will be fired to New York for 35 euro."

Once I got over the feelings of terror the flight was unexpectedly pleasurable, though in trying to write the first draft of this article as I flew, I unfortunately dropped my laptop somewhere over County Meath. Hopefully there was nobody underneath. I have to say the lads at IEA probably won't really get their project off the ground until problems like that are sorted out. However, don't let my experiences deter you from giving IEA a twang.

WHALESONG

Have you noticed that whales have begun behaving a little oddly? A couple of years back we had Orca cavorting in the River Lee; then there was a whale that somehow got stuck in the Firth of the Forth; now according to reports, humpbacks are trying to force their way up the Bandon River. Nobody seems particularly worried, but when a whale starts to submarine up an inland waterway, that's like a human flapping their arms and standing at the top of a skyscraper making tweet-tweet noises. One theory is that radar and sonar signals from shipping are messing with the inner tracking systems of these leviathans. But I personally think that they're just trying to get away from Japanese and Norwegian people bearing harpoons. The smarter whales have decided to disguise themselves as overweight salmon, probably reasoning that the worst that can happen is a fly-impaled top lip. For some years now, these harpoon-dodgers – posing as peel – have been splashing up the Bandon River to spawn, terrifying anglers and getting stuck under some of the smaller bridges. The Government have hushed it up as far as news reportage is concerned - obviously keen to maintain diplomatic relations with Japan to keep up a supply of Toyota's and Nintendo Wii consoles. And antagonising Norway after their last visitation in longboats is unthinkable. Government spokesmen have been putting it all down to an angler's natural tendency to exaggerate the size of the fish they've lost:

"I'm telling ya, it must have weighed at least three tons and it was *this* long:"

Angler paces out fifty metre section of riverbank.

—

Well, last week the blubber hit the fan when two humpbacks became wedged under the arches of a bridge in Murragh. There were all manner of complaints from local farmers who claimed the whales kept them awake half the night with tuneless lugubrious singing.

"Twas like two auld fellers caterwauling after a crate of porter," was how one local put it to me. "T'wouldn't have been so bad if they'd known the bleddy words."

All of this got out only because photographs of the two whales struggling under the bridge with a coach going over the top, were posted in recent weeks on the internet site www.whalespretendingtobesalmon.ie. After this the whole story unravelled: accounts of anglers desperate not to relinquish hold of their rods, waterskiing on their bellies from Innishannon to Enniskeane. Even worse, some of the whales, on reaching the spawning pools around Dunmanway, have been indulging in X-rated behaviour – the problem being that they can't lay eggs and fertilize them like a salmon and so have been trying to reproduce normally in shallow pools. As whales are the largest mammals on earth in more ways than one, Peeping Toms have run screaming from the riverbank, vowing celibacy for life. Meanwhile, research at the other end of the salmon's spawning cycle has suggested that weird whales are causing havoc with Canadian river fauna. Grizzly bears, for instance, who for aeons have stood at the top of waterfalls to snatch migrating salmon, have been particularly hard hit. *Literally.* Bears standing hopefully at the top of their local waterfall, have been head butted by three-ton minke whales leaping from a pool below. Reports suggest that the Grizzly population has been massively demoralised by it all. Understandably, waking up a little peckish and gambolling down to a nearby river for breakfast only to be torpedoed by something the size of a bus with a mouth you could hibernate in, has affected the appetite of many bears. Forest rangers claim thousands of the Grizzlies are depressed and lie cowering in caves with paws over their heads. Teams of volunteers waving large picnic baskets have attempted to entice these Yogis from their lairs to no avail.

Clearly things will only get worse unless a ban on whaling is implemented immediately. And if the government won't get tough with whaling nations, ordinary people should take direct action themselves. Forget petitions. Just write a stiff letter to the Japanese or Norwegian governments and sign it Barack Obama. After all, if a humpback can change their identity, why shouldn't you or I pretend to be President of the United States? Bush did.

A Good Word for the Rain

Rain! Isn't it grand stuff?

You wouldn't announce *that* to a washed out festival or barbecue unless you wanted to be hospitalised by umbrella-wielding mobs. So I generally keep such heretical thoughts to myself. Until recently, that is, when I began to worry.

You see, I believe most rain is pretty friendly. Think of 'mizzle,' that soft mist you see donkeys standing in, stock still. Drifting off a mountainside in fine flurries that tickle the face, it's as pleasurable a form of weather as you are likely to meet: friendly, unassuming, lovable. Yet still everybody hates it *because it's rain*. Fair enough to curse if you're caught in a lashing downpour wearing no more than a bikini (and don't ask what sort of loony woman or even loonier man ventures through a storm clad in two-piece swimwear), but if people are going to blaspheme for being touched with the gentle whifflyness of a new-born bunny's nose, it's obvious that Rain is fighting a prejudice that runs deeper than Sonya O' Sullivan in a coal mine.

Pause for one awful moment and consider where we'd be without all that heavenly drizzling manna. As a subject for polite conversation it's unending. Would we prefer to be left with only *impolite* conversation? Though you listen to the young people and it's certainly the way we're going. Salmon and trout – what would they be swimming in once the rivers dried up? Just the sewage. Consider, if you will stop your vicious black vendetta against precipitation for just a moment: *water.* That's rain without the gaps in between. You can drink ten pints of it, drive 100 miles stone cold sober, and if the guards stop you, face the little breathalysing bag with equanimity. Without water, that other stuff, (which has you arrested after ten pints for driving all over the road), would be a choking mouthful of hops, about as thirst quenching as the Sahara. And who can doubt that most Bedouins poke their heads from a tent of a morning, look up at another dazzling blue sky and turn back to their wives grumbling – *dirty old day*. Bedouins attempting to bathe amidst those baking dunes, have to watch glumly as bubble bath evaporates into hot sand and their rubber ducks melt. They may have lots of oil. But who wants to scrub their back and sing in a bath of Castrol with bars of soap covered in grit? As it stands, the Sahara can only contemplate our rain-induced greenery and be brown with envy, khaki with envy, burnt umber with envy.

Not least, rain as a commodity can be counted on to fall. It very rarely goes up – unlike the price of a pint or foreign holidays in the sun. You know where you stand, even if it's only in a puddle. For heaven's sake we're reputedly 70 per cent water, so we're dissing nearly threequarters of ourselves when we moan about rain. Which brings me back to my worries.

Recently I've been waking in the middle of the night fretting that if everybody keeps dissing those scintillating airborne droplets, Rain will slink off to a country that's more appreciative and we'll be the dry equivalent of sunk.

Either that or it'll maybe rain all the harder out of sheer spleen. I mean how much bitching can the Rain take? It must be fed up with coming down soft, sneaking in an apologetic drizzle over fields, trying to pass itself off as mist, at a loss to understand what is so loathsome about itself. One day soon, it'll overhear two Bedouins on an exchange visit to Cork and discover that in Africa people *dream* of a good drenching and go so far as to *dance* for rain. Our weather will head South, and that'll be it. The scientists will call it global warming. But we'll know it was nothing more than our own bloody ungratefulness.

So maybe we should *whisper confidentially* "Dirty old day", and then announce in stentorian tones: "Rain! Don't you just love it! Oh the wonder of those drops going coldly down the back of my neck. Isn't the sound of that drip coming in through the roof a veritable music to the ears? Ah! The fine odour of damp rising from the back of the press, we are indeed fortunate to be blessed with so much wet. I adore it!"

Perhaps – in the spirit of meteorological diplomacy – we should try and find a silver lining in all the clouds that are hurrying across the Atlantic with the next deluge. Next time you hear clattering fistfuls of rain being thrown against the window, think of it as a natural resource. Poland has its coal. Canada its redwoods, Hawaii its attractive dancing women in hula hula skirts. Ireland has rain. Go out into the garden or street and welcome it with open arms. Sing. Dance and... Hey – I was only.... Ow! Ow! Stop hitting me with those umbrellas!

BAH! NODDY HOLDER!

Finding myself without a tree or Christmas dinner, I set out in the Season of Goodwill attempting to spare a thought for those less well off than me, but then found myself in an overcrowded supermarket aisle listening to a loop tape of Slade's 'Here It Is Merry Xmas' and couldn't think of anyone. Ebenezer Scrooge would have spluttered: Bah!

Noddy Holder! But my yuletide empathy was rescued by a freezer full of twizzlers beside my gridlocked trolley.

'Turkeys," I thought, "they're unequivocally worse off than me. Even *I'm* better looking than a turkey. And at this time of year, the poor fowl do get awful picked on."

You don't have to be a member of the Turkey Liberation Front to concede that being a walking Christmas dinner has its drawbacks come the month of December. In a season when it's nice to be surrounded by those you're close to, what must it be like to find yourself surrounded instead by gravy and only really close to sprouts and spuds? After a narrow escape from the genocide of Thanksgiving, our dangle-nosed friends suddenly find everyone humming "Silent Night" to an accompaniment of knives being scraped across a steel. They must wonder:

"What have we done to deserve this? Was it something we said? That gobbling noise we make doesn't mean: 'We like gobbling so much we want to be gobbled', it means: 'Heeeeelp! I can hear the sound of advent calendars opening!'"

I'm sure as they flap up to turkey heaven, in skeletal flocks, the creatures must muse in mystification: "Feck's sake, why is nobody eating swans?"

And they'd have a point. Why not snatch a free range Christmas dinner as it glides down the River Bandon? Why not 'oven ready' swans? There's plenty of meat on them. They look snowy and Christmassy. I've nothing against swans per se. But if you want a white Christmas they would seem the obvious choice, and a more fitting featherless friend to put on the table and carve to bits.

Given the enormous avian sacrifice that turkeys make to the entire Yuletide experience I feel the very least they deserve is a visit from Santie. But he's probably snowed under in the North Pole with – well, snow and seven billion letters from a population increasing exponentially with every passing December 25th. Last thing he wants is to be deluged by notes saying pretty much the same thing in wobbly illegible writing because the pen is being held in a beak:

'Dear Santie for Xmas this year I'd like – a vote. Or: my life. Or a Christmas dinner in which a large bird doesn't play the starring role.'

Can I just say here *en passant*, that Santie has been a bit of a let-down in recent years. I asked for a million euro in 2008, to be clever, tall and handsome with more hair in 2009. I got books, socks and jumpers. It seems when I was young, back in the early years of the twentieth century, I'd ask for an orange, or spinning top, or new penny farthing and Santie would always come up trumps. Nowadays I unwrap what I hope is a brand new BMW only to find it's beige slippers many sizes too large.

Anyhow, there I was rummaging in frustration through supermarket freezers for a swan, when I looked from a window to see someone purchasing the last tree from what only ten minutes earlier had been a large stack. This happens every year because every year Christmas starts earlier. Folk like me think they've so much time, they'll leave off buying a tree almost indefinitely, and so my family always ends up with the runt of the forest: a wonky asymmetrical mutant that's virtually lost all its needles before the point of purchase and then sheds the rest being dragged from the car and into our front room, where it stands like a nightmarish portent of a planet deluged by sulphuric acid rain. The fairy screams when you stick her on top. Put presents under it and everybody weeps at the sheer tragedy of the spectacle.

Feeling the pressure of being treeless and swanless and with everyone bumping trolleys like dodgem cars, I heard Bing Crosby start up for the four millionth time that he's dreaming of a white Christmas.

"Why?" I hissed into the ether: "Snow is cold. It pushes up winter fuel bills and with the price of oil the way it is and everything else we have to buy to furnish festivities we've barely two spuds to rub together by the time the new year swings around."

As a dislodged tin of shortbread biscuits fell from a top shelf onto my head, it occurred to me that not only would turkeys not vote for christmas, but I wouldn't either. I went cold turkey on the entire tinselly experience and became suddenly in favour of no christmas. No winter. Just summer and the edited highlights of spring and autumn.

Taking a last look into the freezer, I said to the twizzlers:

"You're best out of it guys."

Then made for the car park muttering: "Bah! Noddy Holder!"

I can't see anything restoring my festive spirits but a brand new BMW and a swan leg with lashings of gravy.

LEANING TOWER OF BALLYDEHOB

In recent weeks there's been a bit of ballyhoo in Ballydehob about the tower erected by Eugene Harrington. I knew about the edifice before I saw the photographs in last week's *Southern Star*, as I'd heard two people standing at a bar talking about it:

"Stupid."

"Did you ever hear of anything so stupid. A 500-foot tower made of iron girders in the middle of a field."

"Stupid."

Then there was the letters page and complaints that Harrington's Leaning Tower of Liberty looks like 'a pylon that's been hit by a plane', and that the figurine is an insult to other monuments around the world. I decided I'd better get out there before the tower was torn down. I met Harrington at the foot of what did indeed look like a leaning statue of liberty made out of Meccano, and after peering up in awe, I interviewed him whilst climbing a winding metal staircase to the top of the person shaped pylon. As a blustery wind tore at our clothes and hair I asked what his response was to those who claimed his metal tower was a blot on the West Cork landscape. What about a letter to the newspaper claiming that he'd turned a sight for sore eyes into a site for eyesores?

"The thing people are complaining about..." he shouted over the buffeting gale, "...is that it leans. It's *meant* to lean. Jaysus, that bleddy thing in Pisa has been doing it for years and look at the money they've made. Here we are in the middle of a recession and I say – think of the boost for economy and tourism. At the moment they're struggling to get a single ferry going from Swansea to Cork.

After this is finished, sure there'll be dozens of Cork-Swansea ferries needed for all the people wanting to see it."

"Eugene," I shouted, "what about the complaints that you had no planning permission?"

"The planners don't understand the planning process in this country," he bawled, snatching at his hat before it was gusted from his head. "The correct procedure, and it's always been so, is that a feller builds a house or a barn or a large tourist icon or whatever, and if it's still standing after a couple of years, applies for retrospective planning permission. And they give it because you'll come after them with a shotgun if they don't. Jaysus, how could you tell whether a building will stand up to the wind and rain until it's built? You can make all sorts of plans on fancy bits of paper till the cows come home, but until the walls are up and the roof's on, how will your neighbours know what they're objecting to?"

By this time, we were quite high up. And it was possible to see Ballydehob's brightly coloured houses in the distance. However, I was alarmed by how difficult it was to stay upright in the high wind, with the tower swaying and leaning alarmingly. Eugene didn't seem to notice however and went on shouting:

"There's a lack of vision in this country as far as encouraging tourism is concerned. My brother Tim now, was jailed for introducing lions into the wilderness around Ballydehob. He'd set up a company *West Cork Safari Holidays* and there had been a lot foreign interest, but local farmers were up in arms because they were worried about their stock. Feck's sake. Don't they realise that lions and sabre-toothed tigers were here before us? It's only re-introducing native species. It was an outrage that Tim was jailed when only very few people were eaten and half a dozen cows at most. People came from all over the world to see if they could spot or track down them lions, which brought a lot of money into the country. Folk being eaten, frees up jobs for other people and brings work for undertakers, doctors, florists who make wreaths, and local reporters like yourself. There was a lot of anger about Tim releasing a dozen or so Fer-de-lance snakes – one of the most poisonous snakes in the world. Sure where's the harm? You could be run over by a bus. But nobody's banishing them. 3,000 people killed on the roads last year but one person gets bitten by a snake and there's uproar. A few people go missing, and a couple of human bones are found in a pile of lion dung and people start jumping to all kinds of......"

At this moment, right in the middle of Eugene's fascinating and lucid argument, there was a terrible rending noise as the tower was uprooted and with a loud whistling noise, began to fall.

"....conclusiooooooooooooooons!"

We both screamed to see a green field coming towards us at what seemed like a million miles an hour. If it hadn't been for a soft landing in the deep sludge of Harrington's pond, I wouldn't be here now, dictating this from my bed, with my limbs mummified in plaster and bandages.

GEAROID HILL

Searching for the etymological roots of the word 'hill' on Wikipedia, I discovered the word had its genesis in the name of an unsung local hero: Gearoid Hill. It seems he was born in the middle of the first millennium, possibly around 660, and was mentioned in a number of early chronicles, most notably Bede's 'Historia Ecclesiastica Anglorum'

'Gyrowd Hyll a mann from west Iyrland performs miracles of prodigious strength.' And 'Life is lyke the mound made by Hyll that the sparrow must fly over to reach the other side.'

We often laugh that folk in earlier times believed the world was flat. But in fact, it *was* flatter then, and might have remained so but for the visionary efforts of this one man. For years, Bede's words were dismissed as yet another example of his eccentric belief in miracles. But gradually, with the advent of Creationist theory, geologists have come to reappraise the Venerable Bede's words and conclude that much of our present landscape may have been inspired comparatively recently.

There's good reason to believe Hill was from Munster. A slip of vellum in the illuminated manuscript of the Book of Durrow alludes to: 'The man Hyll who bringeth us all closer to heaven when he maketh mounds in the rains of the southern west'.

Early converts to Christianity, as Hill would have been, often thought that the higher you stood, the closer you were to Heaven. And this may have been what first prompted his astounding feats. Evidence from a little known 7th century poem of Celtic origin, recently unearthed and transcribed from Latin by scholars in Frankfurt University, speaks of a man, dwelling west of Cork, single-handedly inventing the hill – discovering one had appeared behind him whilst digging a ditch in his back garden. If Gearoid was this man, and there will always be controversy and dispute about historical figures from so long ago, the prototype hummock he created may have been no Croagh Patrick, but it was certainly the beginning of a lifelong obsession. Gearoid was inspired to create ever more ambitious humps over the flattened plains of the Irish countryside. Many archeologists and geologists now think some of his early attempts at earth-raising were in the Dunmanway area. They certainly appear a little rough and unfinished in comparison to, say, McGillycuddy's Reeks. But whilst local chieftains must have been impressed by his industrious ability to raise large earthworks as the end results were excellent sites for forts and lookout posts, Hill's endeavours were fraught with difficulty. For at this point, as Bede mentions in his 'Historia', Hill had only invented up and had not properly formulated down.

"They that walk up hylls not knowing down must pray mightily."

This led to people getting stranded at the top of his hummocks and becoming hermits – an ancient corruption of the word *Herbert*. Mercifully for us all, Hill eventually came up with down and his increasingly megalomaniac visions of how soil and rock should be arranged saw him start on McGillycuddy's Reeks around 685 and a few years later, in a fit of enthusiasm whilst on holiday in Westmeath: the Mountains of Mullingar. These were tremendous achievements for one man – especially in the face of violent hostility from many unfit lazy people who preferred the world flat and hated having to struggle breathlessly over the difficult and demanding terrain that Hill was designing. One of the striking similarities between modern Ireland and that of 700AD is that then, as now, many suffered from poor diets. They were unfit and overweight and didn't get enough exercise. This led in 704 to Hill being thrown out of the country by angry and exhausted Dubliners after he created the Wicklow mountains.

Undismayed by this expulsion, he went on to greater things. Travelling first across the Irish Sea he built Snowdon, the Lake District and the Scottish Highlands. Differences in geological formations to his early works suggest that by the time Hill started on Ben Nevis he had a number of assistants laying down the foundations for his artistry in the way that apprentices would be later employed by Renaissance artists such as Leonardo Da Vinci. Whatever, pursued by irate Scotsmen, he fled to the

European mainland where he fashioned such masterpieces as the Alps and the Pyrenees before moving south to fashion his *piece-de-resistance:* Everest. Many think Hill died in Australia trying to carry a large point up Ayers rock. We'll never know.

One of Ireland's unsung heroes, Hill's legacy was a leaner, scrawnier, populace with fewer coronary problems and respiratory diseases. Yet this man who quite literally changed the face of the earth was soon forgotten. At the very least he should be seen as the father of modern landscape gardening – a Capability Brown of the Dark Ages. I'd like to think that the County Council could perhaps scrape together enough money to erect a fitting tribute and memorial to Gearoid in commemoration of his incredible achievements. Surely with all our modern plant equipment we could fix it to honour the man with a small mountain range, some Irish Alps or Celtic Himalayas, between Ballineen and Dunmanway. And place a large statue of him at the top, gazing out intrepidly over the earth.

LAZY SALMON

In recent years the numbers of salmon caught in our rivers has been in decline, causing concern to the tourist industry and fisheries across the country. Overfishing has been blamed, but last week a government spokesman for the environment Mike O'Mahoney, created a storm by claiming that there are actually *more* fish but they're lazier!

O'Mahoney speaking to a gathering of news reporters, had this to say:

"We've been ringing Irish Salmon for the past few years and it's clear from our research that the cause of the trouble is not depleted stocks or overfishing but the fact that the salmon can't be arsed swimming up the rivers or making the trip over the Atlantic any more. It's too much work. They're just hanging round the estuaries – malingering, loitering – causing trouble by picking on the smaller fish like sea trout and that's why a lot of them are ending up in prison."

Amidst sounds of mystification from the audience, a journalist asked for clarification: "Prison?"

"Cages," said O'Mahoney. "In them cages."

"On fish farms you mean?"

"Fish farms, prisons, call them what you like." The minister banged on the table before him. "It's just symptomatic of a malaise that's spreading across Ireland. Lazy young people – you can't get a day's work out of them – wanting life easier and easier. That's why these fish won't go up the rivers. Tis too much like hard work pushing their heads up all that floodwater, jumping up the weirs, it's lazy-good-for-nothing parr and springers who want the Life of Riley and don't give a damn about our tourist industry. When we were young we had to walk to school with no shoes at three in the morning, and who can doubt that the mammy and daddy salmon are telling their kids – we used to have to swim the Atlantic and go flying up the River Shannon, and now ye can't be arsed!"

More noises of consternation arose as well as stifled laughter before another question was posed from the floor:

"Mr O'Mahoney, critics point to your ownership of several large fishing boats, what have you to say to them?"

"Don't talk to me about that! The decline in the numbers of salmon has nothing to do with overfishing! There's plenty of salmon. You could walk on their backs from here to America. They're like young fellers up and down the country. Too lazy to get up out of a sea bed and earn an honest shrimp. They just need a good kick up the back fin!"

A week later, I met Mike on one of his boats in Baltimore, to take up an offer to journalists to go diving off his boat and see indolent salmon for ourselves.

"Good for nothing but seafood platter the lot of them," said Mike as we weighed anchor in Roaringwater Bay. I was handed scuba gear and saw immediately that things had changed since my day when diving apparatus comprised of a copper helmet, lead boots and a long hose attached to an air pump on deck. Still, I sploshed over the side with Mike and we descended only twenty feet, before drifting over numberless multitudes of smolt, looking sulky and uncommunicative on the ocean floor. Comatose amongst the kelp, as far as begoggled eyes could see, the fish lay as if at a vast sleepover, like teenagers unable to rise from bed in the morning, but without the groans. I watched for several minutes, and it seemed pretty clear to me that not one of them had an occupation or was emigrating. Mike swam down, waving his hands and kicking some fishy behinds with his flippers. Seeing bubbles swarm from his mouthpiece, I guessed he was brusquely exhorting the fish to cross the wet and mighty prairie of the Atlantic. I thought this unwise. It's one of the little rules I've made for myself: *Don't go up to gangs of teenagers roaring that they're layabouts who should be swimming the Atlantic whilst delivering penalty kicks up their backsides.* It's asking for trouble. And sure enough, within moments, a mighty murmurating shoal arose. From behind a rock, I watched Mike vanish inside a tornado of smolt and sand. It was one against several million, and not fancying the odds, I pluckily turned and flippered furiously for shore. I wondered if Mike would survive his Piscean duffing, but reasoned, he was a politician, and they're at their most slippery when in deep water. As I clambered panting on my hands and knees onto dry land, after a watery excursion of only a couple of hundred yards, I was much more inclined to see the other side of the argument: just what IS the point of swimming the Atlantic? It's a question many a young salmon must ask themselves. Three thousand miles of briny breaststroke, before leaping up rivers with untreated effluent in the gills. And your reward for all this endeavour? Being swatted onto dry land by a grizzly bear's paw, or brained by a fisherman's priest. Exactly *what* is in it for a young salmon trying to make their way in the world? Spawning? Better surely to wait a few years, then about turn and reproduce in the river you've just swum out of? I began to feel a sneaking respect for all those young salmon lying on ocean beds all day, just doing their own thing. I wanted to wade back into the waves and yell:

Lads, just stay in bed. I wouldn't want to cross the Atlantic either!

But then I figured Mike, if he'd had any sense, would probably have yelled that much, much louder already.

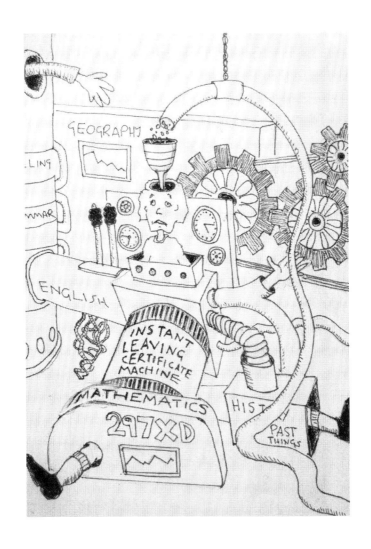

THE TROUBLE WITH MACHINES

I'm testing out a new software programme for Microsoft Windows: *Articulate.* It's basically a software programme for writing articles. You just put in a few facts and key words and it composes essays for you. Whilst the programme is writing this I'm actually lying in a hammock beneath a palm tree in Hawaii being serenaded by beautiful ladies in grass skirts strumming ukuleles. What's more, according to my friends and family, the copy *Articulate* creates is miles better than the rubbish I usually write. The only trouble is that just occasionally the programme starts to *Bertie Ahern put the chocolate up his nose and discussed the giraffes...*if you see what I mean. Which brings me to the topic that I've set this article writing programme to explore: that technology has actually gone too far and is completely out of control and making our lives worse.

Take the car for instance. No, don't, because all the driving around is causing mass obesity and pollution and global warming and if everybody walked I could get into Cork twice as fast because there'd be no other drivers on the road getting in my way. So instead, let's take the automated litter bins that a lot of towns have been installing across the county. Now I dare say they seemed like a great idea at the council meeting: computerised litter bins on legs that walk around picking up rubbish that careless humans have thoughtlessly let flutter to the gutter. These bins, developed from Japanese gaming technology ought to make everybody's lives easier. They can even be programmed to say polite niceties as they wield the pooper scooper:

"Have you finished Fido? Because my foot wants to use that pavement after you."

These amazing machines are a Tidy Towns godsend until that moment when you read reports that automated litter bins have been chasing old people down the street and snatching paper from their hands and lollipops from the mouths of toddlers. Last week, two bins in Durrus started fighting over an empty crisp packet they'd picked up simultaneously. A council spokesman said that the bins were merely programmed incorrectly. But that's my point: *Bertie Ahern put the chocolate up his nose and discussed the giraffes...*Teenagers bully these bins, pushing them over or teasing them by handing them plastic bottles and not letting go until the machine starts to lose its temper and say:

"Let go, you are messing with my motherboard!"
Wouldn't it just be simpler not to drop litter?

Last week I read in a science journal that the Americans had successfully tested a child-educating machine. You drop a five-year-old in one end and they come out the other half an hour later, fully educated with a thorough grasp of the classics and twelve languages and every single point of their leaving cert. Now put aside the fact that such a machine will make us adults look even stupider and would reduce teachers to just reading the start-up manual and flicking a switch, what would happen to the child who *Bertie Ahern put the chocolate up his nose and discussed the giraffes...*I can tell you because one of the sixteen-year-old school drop-outs that scientists used to test the machine, got stuck inside for two days and the results can be seen on YouTube. After the boy's mother finishes ranting about cover-ups and compensation for her son, the poor child speaks for ten minutes thus: *George Washington was the first King of France and he also invented the horse. When Christopher Columbus set out from America to discover France, George was the first person he met when he stepped off the plane. Also seventy-two plus seventy-two makes oxygen.* You see the problem? All this new technology just isn't safe.

In fact, *Articulate* has put forward such a convincing case against technology that when I get back from Hawaii, I'm going to wipe the feckin' programme off my computer and write everything by hand with a quill pen. Because then there won't be any *bottlenose dolphins rampaging through my mashed potatoes whilst Julie Andrews sings 'climb every piano tuner' from inside a tupperware box cunningly concealed underneath Bertie Ahern putting chocolate up his nose whilst discussing the giraffes.*

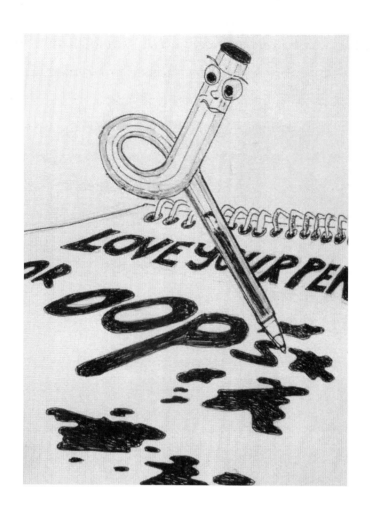

THE SECRET LIFE OF BIROS

Philosophy is often dismissed by ordinary folk as the thinking person's way to avoid hard work. Furrow your brow, weigh your chin on your fist, and tell the family you're cogitating about intractable problems, and there's a fair chance you won't have to do the washing up. We don't know with any certainty that Descartes became a philosopher to wriggle out of emptying the latrine or digging ditches, but lying on a couch staring into space, surrounded by attentive servants, must have seemed an easier option in 1600 than loading dung onto a cart with a pitchfork. So it was with great interest that I went to interview Professor Stephen McQuitty at UCC. His book: *The Secret Life of Biros* has rocked academics across the globe with the idea that philosophy should be practical, useful with measurable benefits for mankind. Seated in his office on campus, surrounded by a formidable library, this distinguished pipe-smoking professor spoke to me about his revolutionary theory.

IW: Professor McQuitty, your ideas have upset many people in philosophical circles.

MCQUITTY: Well, yes. I set out initially to solve a simple everyday problem that has baffled eminent scientists, philosophers and dry cleaners for decades – why do ballpoint pens only leak when they get in your pocket? And after wrestling with this sticky blue-fingered dilemma for several years, I came to conclusions that literally blew the mind.

Here he laid down his pipe on a mahogany table and looked up into the air thoughtfully.

MCQUITTY: I began by studying Bics. For six months I watched one as it lay on a table, motionless and inscrutable. Nothing happened. Undeterred, I then filmed a biro in laboratory conditions for a year and it still didn't leak a drop. In the end I popped it in my pocket and went down to a lecture and within five minutes my suit looked like it had been attacked by a large squid.

IW: In your book you claim that they actually *know* when they've been dropped into a pocket.

MCQUITTY: Oh yes. You can throw them across a room, artificially agitate them in darkened conditions without a leakage of any kind. But the moment they get in your jacket they'll squirt.

IW: And you think this proves they are an intelligent life form?

MCQUITTY: Without question. Have you noticed the way they prefer the new or expensive jacket, especially in white or cream?

IW: Which has led you professor, to speculate on the inner spiritual life of the biro?

MCQUITTY: Yes, despite great conformity in appearance, biros are obviously rebels. They're pushed around all their lives. They pretty much have to write what they're told in the iron fist of their owner. They're plastic slaves and they know it. Their one chance to rebel against their owners is to ruin a good coat forever by leaving a dark blue stain in the corner of a pocket that no amount of dry cleaning can remove. Sadly, this act of noble defiance is often their last. Much like a bee that dies after using its sting, the biro – oonce having squirted cathartically – is defunct. It will never write again.

IW: It is perhaps your conclusions surrounding the intimate relationships we have with biros that have caused most controversy. Could you elaborate on them?

MCQUITTY: Accept that your biro has feelings. Talk to your pen. Treat it with respect. Don't throw it down on the desk when you're angry. Tell it several times a day that you love it and respect it and value its company and then just to be on the safe side, put it in a plastic bag if you *do* put it in your pocket.

IW: Professor, there are those in the academic community who question the validity of your work. Who wonder if this kind of research is really philosophy at all and who ask if studying the inner life of a biro is the sort of thing we should be throwing public money at. What would you say to them?

MCQUITTY: I'd tell them that Descartes' entire philosophical works were about the biro and his most famous lines have been wilfully misconstrued by scholars. It should read: *I ink therefore I am,* and anyone who tells you differently is an anti-biro, pen-hating idiot who probably wants to tell lies about my organisation, the Pen Liberation Front.

At this point, the Professor – a mild and amiable man for the earlier part of our interview – became extremely animated and red-faced. He began to shout loudly and I crept out of his office, fearing that he might become violent. The last words I heard him shout as I hurried away down the corridor were:

MCQUITTY: Pens are equal to humans, *superior* in fact. Many great people in History were pens! Caesar was retractable and used his nose as a nib...Where would Shakespeare have been without a quill?

One might be tempted to laugh at the Professor's ideas, but on reaching home, I found the pen I'd been taking notes with, had leaked disastrously in my jacket pocket. I've been talking secretly to biros ever since – just in case.

HEARING AID

As you know, this column likes to keep on top of all the latest technology. I'm a bit of a frustrated inventor at heart. Frustrated, because most of my inventions never quite get off the ground. Though as I explain to anyone who will listen, if Orville and Wilbur Wright had let their frustrations get the better of them, someone else would have invented the aeroplane six months later and got all the credit. So it's important to get in first, however catastrophically impractical your blueprints. In the spirit of which, I thought I'd better patent a little idea for a new type of hearing aid in these pages – of which I've been meaning to speak for some weeks. But for reasons that will become clear, have been unable to.

Now, it's long been the assertion of my family that I talk too much. Not so much the gift of the gab as being cursed with a lack of taciturnity. They claim I will talk to anyone or anything. Random strangers, the cat, the dog, myself, even inanimate objects. And we don't even have a dog. They claim that I can be found in an empty room talking to the television, even shouting at it when a football match is on. Even at times conducting a one-man choral society with the shower. It's all true, though I say in my defence, some people talk to their plants and there's many an item of furniture or fitting that might be more intelligent than they let on. Heaven knows what the furniture is thinking as it looks on at all the shenanigans that go on in the average human household. It might only be profound politeness that prevents the furniture from passing comment. Though our sofa always utters a loud 'ouf' when somebody parks down on it after a heavy meal, and just occasionally "feck's sake, would you ever lose a few pounds like?"

Just because something doesn't speak doesn't mean it's not a sentient thinking being – I told my wife. It might just be a good listener. And she replied that just because something speaks doesn't mean it isn't an unintelligent blockhead. Anyhow, that's all by the by. The point of this little literary excursion into ululation and aural attending is that I'd found myself going a little deaf over the past few years, and in the middle of the night came up with a solution that I thought would beget the family fortune and make it unnecessary to send the children out begging from door to door. All it involved was a drill and a steady hand. I bounded down from the landing at the top of the stairs where I sleep and was surprised to find my family solemnly gathered around the kitchen table, upon which was a small parcel.

Happy birthday! They chorused.

I'd totally forgotten that about this time of year I am twenty-eight, and fell upon the gift-wrapped gift. It was a very dapper, spotted cotton scarf. Lo and behold, if for my birthday they hadn't bought me a gag! Perhaps they were thinking as much for themselves as for me, such as when you buy your spouse a Manchester United DVD for Christmas. They knotted it round the back of my head, and then amazingly, everything went quiet. For the first time in years, I could actually hear what other people were saying in the room. Amazing. So this is my invention – you might say it is not mine, but a yoke my family stumbled across first. Ah! But I first saw the potential in this piece of technological wizardry. How many millions down the ages saw lightning before Ben Franklin ran up a harness for electricity? So, no need for a drill and a steady hand. I've patented the tea towel instead. After all, how many can run to double figures in the Euro department for a polka dot scarf muzzle. And that's about the size of it. If you want to improve your hearing, you don't need any of these fancy machines that lodge in the ears. Just get the missus to tie a bit of old tea towel round your mouth and knot it at the neck then listen to the difference. If you want to hear better, *just shut up!*

Trans-Ireland Moustache

Ah yes, the financial crisis. There I was minding my own business when all of a sudden I 'owed' 80,000 euro to mega-rich bondholders. Now I'm constantly being woken in the middle of the night by my wallet sobbing that it feels empty and that it's fed up of being upended and desperately shaken. I long to know the identity of these Bondholders so that I might saunter up to one of them in the Ritz or wherever they hang out and say:

"Excuse me. Stop eating that lobster and caviar for a moment. My wallet is very upset. There are many wallets like mine in Ireland that seem to owe 80,000 euro each to prop up banks for some dodgy speculation you were involved in. How's about emptying *your* wallet – yes that ebullient leather monster that seems to have an insatiable appetite for Irish taxpayer's money – so that we can all go back to having jobs and public services. And if that means you wind up eating jam sandwiches in a transport caff, well..." Alas, this won't happen, because no bondholder would currently dare to pop up from behind their chaise-longue and say *yoo-hoo – over here*. But it set me thinking: two can play at hiding behind the sofa.

Now obviously, any sensible person faced with large debts they are reluctant to dig deep into the pockets for, will lie low. Change their identity. Disguise themselves with a straw boater, facial hair and pretend to smoke a pipe. But might it not be possible to do this on a national scale? I hear you hoot: "*What?* Disguise all of Ireland? Go *nationally* incognito?" Bear with me. Don't laugh and cast the paper over your shoulder braying "the man's mad!" Remember it's *this* or 80,000 a household. My modest and practical suggestion is that we should pretend to be Iceland.

You see, adopting 'Iceland' as a nom-de-plume would involve no great effort, no vast Soviet-like five-year plan? We merely scratch out the R in Ireland and replace it with a C. Many a creditor can be shown the door because they have a bill addressed to the wrong name.

Pretending to be Iceland would also be cool. Well, alright, cold. Not existing on the edge of the arctic circle, we might have to turn off the central heating in winter to get our teeth authentically chattering and introduce a few polar bears into the wild. We could rechristen Dublin 'Reykjavik', scribble 'Krona' over our euro notes in felt pen and all bleach our hair blonde, no problem. There wouldn't be a lot of cultural changes as we're already listening to Bjork and digesting interminable sagas – the economic crisis saga being already harder to swallow than *The Passion Hymns of Hallgrimur Pètursson.* It might help to learn a few Icelandic words. Just eight really. Something like: *"Nei Við höfum engar peningar fyrir þér kveðja"* (No, we don't have any money for you. Goodbye.) The very worst that could happen is we might have to eat Hakari – beheaded shark that's been buried underground for a couple of months.

I don't deny we'd need changes in the landscape. But how much would it cost to bore some big holes in the Wicklow mountains and conceal smoke machines at the bottom to make the country seem a bit more volcanically and geologically active? Not 80,000 per household. Catapult a few tons of cinders from the holes now and then and talk up an ash-cloud to ground planes across the entirety of European airspace and we'd be halfway there. With the winters we've been having, we wouldn't even have to paint the fields white. As an added precaution we could build a large trans-Ireland moustache: blonde, dropped-handlebar lip whiskers, unmistakably Nordic in appearance. This would extend from Dublin to Galway and droop down to the ring of Kerry on one side and the Wicklow mountains on the other. Being 150 miles wide, 5 miles deep and constructed from millions of straw bales shaped to look like a shaggy moustache, the project would provide massive employment opportunities. Satellites looking down (because the EU are wondering where we've got to) or IMF henchmen arriving by air, would be completely flummoxed by the nation's impenetrable disguise.

Just imagine those IMF or EU heavies landing in Dublin's Reykjavik airport. They step off the plane to see a man dressed as Viking Chief Ingōlfur Arnason, one of the first Icelandic settlers, sinking a double-headed axe very deep into a negotiating table and bawling: *"Nei Við höfum engar peningar fyrir þér kveðja."* Because Icelanders don't take any crap, you see. They recently voted in a referendum to let their bondholders burn. Which means – and here's the big payoff – if we pretend to be them, *we can do the same!*

As a practical solution to the nation's woes I really can't see where objections would come from. My solution is cheap and more craic than the alternatives. It's the kind of practical action that ordinary people want: something that doesn't involve marching – which causes blisters and fatigued legs – and spreads a little happiness. Not least, to our wallets.

A DAY AT THE RACES

As travel is said to broaden the mind, I usually avoid it. All these foreign holidays can spread your brains perilously thin.

"And what better vacation than a chair at the bottom of the garden?" I ask Mrs. Wild every summer, as the rain teems down. Her answer is always to fling the irons at me. So on getting into the car to visit a Point-to-Point, I invited my dear wife along to experience the thrills of the chase, reasoning that if I took her to the races one Sunday afternoon, I could argue we'd already been on holiday this summer, which would reduce wear and tear on the wallet and keep the grey matter thick.

Now horse racing and I live in humble ignorance of each other. For most of my life, I've believed that all you need to know about a horse is which end provides garden manure and which end bites, then keep well away from both. So understandably, many things about Point-to-Point puzzled me profoundly. For a start, so many bookies! Three long unshaven lines of them stood on boxes beneath dripping umbrellas, praying for the sun to come out and for showers of money instead. Leaving my wife to gamble away our life savings (fifty-three euro) on horses with the nicest names and jockeys wearing the most harmonizing colours, I ambled off and was innocently inspecting a fine hedge connecting two wooden rails when to my horror a thunder of hooves sounded from behind and stampeding horses bore down on me like a cavalry charge.

"Get off the track ya fool!" some feller in a large fluorescent waistcoat screamed.

I'm telling you, I had to run pretty fast and jump eleven fences to escape from them. And after I got back I was presented with a cup. But that's by the by.

I was looking for Mrs Wild, knowing she wouldn't be far from the Ladies toilets, when I heard a whinnying voice call from the 4x4 and trailer enclosure.

"Hey mister..."

Now, I wasn't particularly surprised to hear a horse talk, they're very intelligent creatures by all accounts. Especially in comparison to some of the people I went to school with. No, I was more surprised to see him smoking a cigarette.

"Have you got a light?"

To be honest, I was a bit shocked. Surely race horses are athletes? To find them taking drugs just like their human counterparts was a bit depressing. And I said as much to his trainer, Ger Duffy who was struggling with a lighter.

"Ah now, a drop of porter and a smoke before a race does no harm. Settles the nerves."

In truth the horse did seem a tad anxious.

"There's some big fellers out there," he neighed. "The other horses I mean. I'm never gonna beat them am I? Why don't we go to the beer tent and see what's coming out the taps instead?"

Ger was having none of this.

"There you go again," he remonstrated, finally lighting the horse's smoke. "Talking like a Shetland pony lining up for the Grand National."

"But have you seen the size of some of the fences? I'll never get over them. Not with some big fat feller on me back."

"It won't be a feller, it'll be a lady."

The horse looked shocked.

"A lady. How can I win with one of them driving?"

"I've entered you for the ladies' race."

"Whoah." He spat out the cigarette and crushed it under a mighty hoof, "That's beneath me dignity. I'm telling ye, human mares whipping me round a course is not my idea of how the world should be organized."

I was just about to step in and urge the animal to remove its chauvinist blinkers when the jockey showed up. The Houyhnhnm was still digging in his hooves as the start of the race was called and his feminine mount hopped on board:

"Us riding people and driving ye round in trailers called 'human boxes' is more like it. Humans leaping over fences with thoroughbreds like me on their backs. A lot of horses would pay good hay and oats to see that."

A whip was applied and horse and rider skittered towards the paddock. I was about to follow and watch the race, when my arm was tugged by Mrs. Wild, beaming from ear to ear.

"I've just won 3,000 euro on a horse called Benidorm, ridden by that nice man from the travel agents." she said.

I suppose I should have been pleased, but I had a dispiriting premonition that my mind, like that of a certain equine steeplechaser, would soon, alas, be broadening.

THE FUNNIEST MAN ON EARTH

It's not often I manage to squeeze a bit of humour into this column, as regular readers will know only too well. My attempts at levity usually attract a long red line of editorial pen underscored with a terse note saying: *Just stick to the facts, Ian.* So I ought to have been delighted last week, when dispatched to interview Stanley Accrington the self-styled *Funniest Man On Earth*. West Cork is the last stop of a barnstorming world-tour for a stand-up who was described by New York's *What's On*, as a comedian who couldn't have fallen flatter if he'd been pushed from the top of the Empire State Building. The tour featured bust ups with three managers, a wife, an airline company, and most of his audiences – not to mention a fracas in which he assaulted his own police protection until police protection was eventually sought for the police protection. With all of this hauntingly to the fore of my mind, I approached meeting Stanley, with the reluctance of a vertigo sufferer being invited into a hot air balloon. We met in a cafeteria off Patrick Street, and shook hands. Feeling returned to my fingers later the next day. I had been expecting a man with the build and demeanour of a nightclub bouncer recently released from Dartmoor, but Stanley was much more intimidating than that: resembling one of the Kray twins and crammed into a suit so tight, one suspected the other twin was also in there as well. He possessed the sort of unflinching stare that would come in useful were the owner also a lighthouse.

"So Stanley," I asked politely, "what makes you so incredibly funny?'

He replied in a Lancashire accent as broad and as unremittingly flat as Morecambe Bay.

"My delivery. My......" Here there was a ten second pause. "... timing. My jokes."

With a titter of encouragement, I asked if I might hear one of the latter. Stanley raspingly cleared some rubble from his throat.

"Why did the chicken cross the road?"

"I don't know Stanley. Why?"

"Cos I gave it *both* barrels of me shotgun instead of one."

I forced a smile.

"Stanley,' I gave a nervous simper, "does it ever bother you if nobody laughs?"

'Not really," he grunted, "if they don't laugh, they've got no sense of humour have they? I'm ahead of me time. Nobody laughed at Beethoven or Van Gogh, but look at them now."

I thought it prudent to move on. All celebrities like talking about how they made it to the top, and I hoped Stanley's biographical history wouldn't require any of my badly-canned laughter.

"Before you turned to comedy you were a lion tamer. Has that helped you?"

"Course it has. Basically, all audiences are vicious animals. Anyone can make 'em roar but sometimes you have to stick a chair in their teeth to get out alive."

To my alarm, he picked up a chair and mimed forcing it down the throat of an enraged audience member. As if I was in the front row.

"You're referring here,' I said mopping my brow with a handkerchief, 'to your recent gig in America where you were nearly beaten to death by an irate audience?"

"Yeah. Cos of me dead animals joke. I asked if anyone had had a pet die recently and when they put their hand up, I laughed. Like I say, to get out I had to run up a few dentist's bills."

"Where did you learn your very idiosyncratic approach to comedy?"

"From me elder brother. He'd tell a joke and then hit me till I laughed. He liked knockabout humour did our Bert."

I could feel the interview drawing to a close even though it had only just started.

"Well, I've time for one more Stanley," I said, feigning enthusiasm.

"Okay. Why did the chicken cross the road?"

"I don't know Stanley. Why?"

"Cos I gave it *both* barrels of me shotgun instead of one."

I was a little nonplussed.

"You've er... told me that one."

"You only need one if it's funny. So laugh."

"But I've heard it already."

His brows darkened.

"I've told that to people thirty times and had them in stitches. So many, the doctors ran out of thread." Stanley suddenly reached over the table and grabbed me by the throat. *"So laugh!"*

"Ow! Ow! Arrgghgggh!" I gurgled, "*hahahahahaha.*"

He released his grip and I fell back into a chair still desperately manufacturing mirth. A faint smile crossed his granite face.

"See. I told you it were funny."

GENETICALLY MODIFIED CARS

It's well known that Ballinscarthy is the birthplace of Henry Ford, who almost single-handedly engineered the twentieth century's love affair with cars by introducing mass-production. What is less well known is that Ford's successor currently lives in West Cork and plans to supercede the petrol engine, by starting an entirely new love affair – w*ith hay.*

Earlier this month I visited the farm of Bart O'Grady, who recently won the coveted Green Science Prize for his research on genetically modified cars. A Trinity graduate who specializes in biodynamic technology, Bart explained his ideas before taking me round his farmland,

"Technology's moving so fast. It's calculated that by 2080, many people will be more machine than human. As the body wears out, new parts will be grown artificially and implanted. Already we have pacemakers, artificial limbs and retinas. Alongside this the unravelling of DNA codes and advances in molecular nanotechnology have made it possible to construct living objects atom-by-atom. My work is merely a bringing together of these advances to solve urgent ecological problems – an attempt to genetically engineer a car that runs on grass and water."

He led me out to some large polytunnels.

"It's now possible to grow machines and create a green car that gets its horsepower, literally from the DNA of a horse implanted using biomechanics, in seed. This is the ultimate green technology: organic plant machinery, spliced with a rootstock of animal genes."

We stepped into the first polytunnel and I saw rows of plants bearing small twitching fruit, that proved to be, on closer inspection, tiny green cars, like dinky toys on stems. Bart bent and let one run on his hands. It made a tiny but discernable whinnying noise.

"The Government is trying to cut CO_2 emissions by introducing electric cars which are fine so far as they go – about 15 kilometres. But building and running them still consumes electricity that comes mainly from fossil fuels. Whereas, my plant machinery needs only a bit of land and fertilizer. Six months after seeding you have a family saloon that consumes a trough of water supplemented with a little fresh hay or grass. You can actually use them as a lawnmower. And it will run all day. There are people who claim we are playing God. But throughout history, man has altered plants and animals genetically to improve them. The modern apple comes from a crab. In early days you were eating them with the pincers still on, fresh out of the sea. Now they grow on trees as Granny Smiths."

I stared down at tiny cars, plainly alive, like little jumping beans, each attached to a leafy green stem.

"I grow them under plastic," Bart explained, "because too much rain and they get blighted by rust."

Our next stop was a converted stable block that is now a garage for full grown specimens that have ripened in Bart's polytunnels before being harvested. Opening a set of double doors, Bart introduced me to a large green automobile with rubbery looking bumpers that were tearing wisps of hay from a bale. The headlamps blinked and stared at us.

"This is Henry, the one we took onto *Top Gear*."

I circled a sporty convertible in amazement, because it was palpably alive, like a horse.

Bart opened a door and ushered me into the passenger seat.

"We'll go for a quick spin." He said sitting beside me, "No keys. Just enter the password, which a voice recognition programme receives as an ignition signal. In this case it's *giddy up*."

At which the exhaust gave loud neighs and the front end reared.

"Jeremy Clarkson loved it."

I could see why. We shot down the drive at 70 mph, Bart wrestling with the steering wheel, tugging at it like reins.

"Incredible to be driving along in a sentient creature," the inventor shouted as we tore along the highway at a frightening velocity. "A living being whose parts can be re-grown and replaced after a crash."

Unfortunately, at this point we passed a gymkhana. The car's headlights took one look at candy-stick jumps and horse boxes to my left and literally leapt from the road with a loud whinny of recognition.

"Whoagghghg! Henry! No!" Bart yelled, wrestling with the steering wheel.

The car drove straight at a stone wall and leapt over it, six feet into the air. We were nearly thrown from our seats. I screamed as if enduring a particularly harrowing fairground ride. Horses, riders and knots of onlookers scattered in astonishment and horror, stampeding to safety behind hot dog stalls as Henry proceeded to tear around the jumps at fifty miles an hour leaping over several, but just crashing through the wall jump and refusing the water to drink it. At this moment I pinged off the seat belt, clambered from the vehicle and ran to safety. Bart got out too, slapping the bonnet of Henry with pride, whilst the car drank thirstily.

"Don't forget to tell your readers," Bart shouted after me, "they can buy it in any colour they want – so long as it's green."

There's nothing stranger

THAN THINGS THAT AREN'T

One of the strange things about being a roving reporter in West Cork searching for the odd and extraordinary is the amount of people who get in touch with me to come and look at something strange when it isn't. Take Billy McMurphy – a farmer from Innishannon. He called me out to hear his singing cow.

"She has the most wonderful voice you ever heard. Operatic I'd call it. Better than Cara O'Sullivan. All I have to do is stand in her field with my piano accordion and play Amazing Grace or All Kinds of Everything and she'll start to sing along, perfectly in key."

Not wanting to miss this sensational milk-producing vocalist I hopped into my car and tore along to his farm. We tramped out over five or six muddy fields until we reached a large herd of cows.

"There she is," he said pointing to a cud-munching Friesian.

He started playing 'Muirshin Durkin' and the cow just looked at us as if we were nuts.

"Come on ya daft bitch."

She began to walk away, grazing. Billy followed her giving a rendition of 'Waltzing Mathilda' at which the cow turned and began to moo loudly – closer to a boo than a moo.

"There ye go," said Billy triumphantly.

"But Billy," I demurred, "that was just a cow mooing."

"Not at all, she was singing clear enough for all to hear."

I felt I had to be frank:

"To be honest it did just sound like an ordinary moo to me."

At which Billy became a bit indignant:

"What do you know about singing? You're probably tone deaf. You've no ear. The amount of tone-deaf people I have coming out to listen to Betsy is almost as amazing as the cow herself. Just listen carefully and you'll hear her singing the tune."

He began squeezing out Carmen's Toreador song on the piano accordion. Betsy mooed at him again, as if telling him in cow language to shut up and go away.

"There you go. Jaysus, the least you could do is applaud her."

"But Billy, it's just mooing, honest."

This made him pretty angry.

"Ah that's it! If ye won't listen! I'm fed up of bringing people out here to share the miracle of Betsy's voice. No way now will you ever get to see my barn dancing chickens."

Billy stumped off muttering.

Then there was a phone call in the middle of the night from a man who drove cars.

"Hello."

"Hello."

"Are you the geezer who does the *Anything Strange* thing in the *Star?*"

"Er, yeah. It's four in the morning you know."

"Yeah, yeah, but listen, my name's John and I drive a car."

"Yes. *And.....?*"

"Well I'm inside it now and it's going along a road."

"So....?"

"Well, I thought maybe you could interview me about it?"

"Why?"

"Because it's strange."

"What's strange about driving a car?"

"Well I'm driving everywhere in reverse."

"Why?"

"So that I'm strange enough to interview. And I'm doing it at four in the morning so that I don't crash into anybody. So go on. Ask me some questions."

"But," I pointed out – it *was* four in the morning – "if you're only driving in reverse to be strange enough to be interviewed, it's not the driving in reverse that's strange, *it's you.*"

At which point there was a loud yell, and a confused banging sound.

"Hallo John?"

The vehicle had obviously crashed. The phone went dead. John didn't go dead however, because he phoned me again a few weeks later, asking me to interview him for wearing odd socks.

And then there was the time I was called out to look at a sheep.

"It's just a sheep." I said. "Doesn't it dance or knit itself or play monopoly?"

"No," said its owner, "It's just a normal sheep. But imagine now, they were very rare, and this was the only one left in the world, and you'd never ever seen one before – not even a picture. Wouldn't you say, seeing this creature for the first time, that it looked more than a little strange?"

And I had to admit this was true. If you'd never met one before, a sheep would look strange. And so would we all. Which only goes to prove, I suppose, that there's nothing stranger than things that aren't.

LEONARDO

PREVIOUSLY UNDISCOVERED SKETCH

Last year, West Cork art dealer – Brad Murphy – came across a previously undiscovered self-portrait by Leonardo da Vinci. An astonishing find. Facsimiles of the original were published in newspapers and art journals across the world.

"There I was, y'know," Brad told me when we met up last week in Cork Opera House, "rooting through some bins behind my local antique shop and this sketch was there, pretty knocked about but I recognised the signature immediately. As we know, Leonardo was a versatile guy: Art, flying machines, backwards writing. The discovery of this piece shows that he attempted to entertain the Medici's with Renaissance comedy sketches that were centuries ahead of their time."

Brad showed me a photograph of the original. It was covered in weird doodles of planets, sinewy body parts and 15th century designs for tumble dryers. The writing was of course Italian in need of a mirror.

"Don't worry if you can't read it," Brad said reassuringly, "the rehearsal of this previously unperformed masterpiece that you will be privileged to see today, is in translation, and none of the sentences will be spoken backwards. Though the actors both speak in Italian accents. Despite this, you'll be hearing an autobiographical sketch pretty much as it was written 500 years ago."

It was a mind-blowing thought. Seated in the front row of the Opera House for the first rehearsed run through, I was entranced to see Leonardo's vision brought to life by two modern day actors who took to the stage in flowing gowns, strange hats and tights. The scene was clearly that of Mona Lisa being painted by Leonardo.

Mona: Leonardo. Can we take a break? Holding this weird smile is killing my face.

Leonardo: Just another five minutes Mona. I'm just filling in all the number fives with the same colour paint.

Mona: It's no good. I can't hold the smile any longer!

(SOUND EFFECT OF GLASS SHATTERING AND THE PIECES FALLING ON THE FLOOR.)

Leonardo: Mona! Your teeth!

Mona: What a mess! Where's the dustpan and brush?

Leonardo: I'm using the brush for your portrait. But you can have the dustpan.

Mona: My smile is ruined. Look at the gaps in my teeth.

Leonardo: Fortunately Mona, I am a Renaissance Man. I can turn my hand to pretty much anything.

Mona: You mean.... you're a dentist too?

Leonardo: No. It means I can write a song about your smile instead and play it on the lute.

Here the actor took up and instrument and played a plangent madrigal.

Leonardo: (SINGS)

      Mona's smile lies in a pile

      of broken white enamel

Her upper occlusals bust.

Her gnashers bit the dust

Now doodlers and drawers

who immortalise her gnawers

must fill her grin in

with crosshatching

"Brad," I said after applauding the actors offstage, "the manuscript appears to end there a little inconclusively?"

Brad sat beside me, rubbing his hands together with conviction and enthusiasm.

"Yeah. Obviously he couldn't find a punchline and so he decided to paint her instead. Though this sketch throws light on a possible reason for the enigmatic nature of Mona Lisa's smile – she was trying to hide the gaps in her teeth."

"Do you think audiences will be happy to pay 40 euro a ticket to see such a short unfinished sketch?"

"Without question. This is a premiere. It's history. Seeing the first performance would almost be like owning the sketch yourself."

"And how much is this sketch worth?" I ventured to ask.

Brad rasped the stubble on his chin in momentary contemplation.

"Well, I'm open to offers of over 10 million really."

IDENTITY THEFT

According to government statistics issued last month, a new more sinister form of identity theft is on the up. The criminals don't just steal your pin numbers and credit cards – they steal your entire existence. Apparently it's a simple matter of leaving your back door unlocked when you go out to get the messages. Whilst you're out someone sneaks in, but instead of lifting the mattress and taking out your savings, which is at least a straightforward decent form of dishonesty, these modern crooks rifle your wardrobe, don your clothes and make themselves a cup of tea. The victim returns from the shops to find a complete stranger sat in the comfiest chair watching the TV and shouting dismissively:

"Out of my house! You've some cheek, walking in here without so much as ringing the doorbell. Don't argue! I don't want to buy anything! I don't like you door-to-door salesmen one bit!"

Hundreds of people all over the country can attest to the fact that if someone takes over your house and pretends to be you, it can be very hard to prove they're not.

Seemingly, identity thieves target lonely people without many friends. Mrs Lilian Hegarty from Kenmare was recently turned from her own front door and left bereft of an identity when a fraudster entered her house whilst she was pegging out the washing and refused to let her back in.

"The trouble was that I'm a bit of an aul recluse, so nobody knew me anyhow. Not even the gards when I went into town to complain. They came up to interview this person claiming to be me, but twas just this chancer's word against mine. The gards said the other person was in possession of the house and possession is 9/10's of the law. I had no means of identification you see. If the thief's wig hadn't suddenly blown off in the wind the Sergeant would never have realised twas a man dressed up in my clothes and pretending to be me."

John O'Mahoney lost his farm and land when four identity thieves entered his house, all pretending to be him. "Sat round my kitchen table all wearing my clothes, they was very convincing. I said twas impossible for there to be four of me, but it was hard to argue with them, because you're just arguing with yourself. The conversation became mighty confusing."

"You can't be coming in here claiming to be one of us, John," they said. "Five John O'Mahoney's is too many altogether. There's barely room in the house for four of me as it is. Sure, we'd never all fit in the one bed."

"In the end I went, because it was four against one. They told me not to go to the gards because I'd only be getting myself arrested. Four times over. They was four times cleverer than me I suppose, which would explain how they got away with it."

Frank McPhee reported an identity theft in Bandon last week.

"I got home and there's a feller there who looked a bit like me, wearing me own clothes. Me wife said she didn't recognise me. Neither did the children. Okay I spent a lot of time in the pub and this feller was a bit better looking than me, but there should be a national clampdown on this sort of thing."

It was later discovered that Frank had actually walked into the wrong house under the influence of alcohol. Still – the fact remains that these crimes are becoming more common and extreme with every passing minute. The most horrifying story belonged to farmer Joe Daly of Wexford, who returned home from his fields to find one of his own cows sitting in his chair reading the paper and claiming to be him.

"I'm telling ya, this cow is a brilliant impressionist. My own wife couldn't tell us apart. There was Buttercup, dressed in my overalls, reading the racing news. Sure if it hadn't been for the horns – which I don't have – and the fact that she said her words with a bit of a moo, I'd have been turned out into the pasture to eat grass instead of her."

So, the message is this; if you go out, lock your doors and take all your clothes with you in suitcases. Even if you're just nipping out to peg some sheets on the line. Because the chances are, there's someone out there wanting to be you. In the meantime, I have a feeling this article is being written by someone else. But that's alright, I can pop down to the pub whilst they're finishing it off and then when I get back....

hey wait a minute ...

Russian Weather Machine

I don't know if anyone has noticed the weather. The black ice or rain that's been falling non-stop for the past few years where summer should be, and it's all the fault of Russian Weather Machines. How do I know? Well I found one in my back garden. Let me explain.

My garden is large and rather overgrown. It is overgrown *because* it's large. Occasionally I wonder if employing a gardener would help, but we really need something more in the line of Dr. Livingstone. I daren't venture beyond the washing line for fear of being eaten by leopards or falling into the maw of a giant Venus flytrap. Unfortunately, every now and then my wife thinks I should do something constructive instead of reading the sports pages and watching her wash up. She pushes me out of the back door with a bucket of sharp implements and tells me I can't come back in until I've found the lawn. Last week, such a fate befell me. For long moments I stood in a monsoon, clacking a pair of shears at a threatening gang of nettles, then I began to hack randomly at some of the more defenceless vegetation. I'd successfully massacred a patch of man-eating daisies when there was a loud rustling and a raggedy granddad with a white beard that reached to his knees burst from a spray of foliage. With hands held high he surrendered a rusty console whilst screaming in Russian: *No shoot Yankee soldier.* Of course, I knew what he was saying because I sing fluent Russian.

Yes, you read that correctly. I sing fluent Russian because my mother played music to me in the womb. Unfortunately, in those days nobody knew it should be

Mozart's more serene and uplifting compositions and she played me Russian opera instead. My formative months were spent listening to Mussorgsky through amniotic fluid reverberating with the more lugubrious arias of *Boris Gudonuv*. Which meant that I emerged nine months later with a deep depression and a tendency to sob in a declamatory manner from my pram. It was years before my parents realised that my early goo goos and gaa gaas were in fact highly articulate demands for a bottle and rusks in a Muscovite operatic argot. Anyhow, faced with a shears-clacking baritone singing in Slav: "What are you doing in my hydrangeas?" the soldier fainted and dropped an ancient device that looked like a dashboard ripped from a crashed Lada. I picked it up, twiddled a dial, and the rain abruptly stopped.

Half an hour later Lev revealed (over a samovar of Barry's) that he was one of hundreds of soldiers with handheld weather machines the Russians parachuted into Europe during the Cold War. The Kremlin planned to destabilize western democracies by making everyone depressed with continuous rainfall. However, Soviet craftsmanship being what it was, most of those dropped onto mainland Europe were carrying defective apparatus. By an oversight, early models dropped on Greece and Spain had only one setting – hot. Ireland being the most farflung

European outpost and last hit by meteorological fifth columnists, unfortunately received new post-sputnik equipment. Hidden in bogs, ditches and gorse bushes the operators were never informed that the Cold War was over and many weather machines are still operating in rural areas. Lev, poor guy, had been in our drizzly back garden since 1958 feeding on compost scraps, until eventually, fed up of a diet of baked beans on porridge, he gave himself up.

And so, after listening to *Boris Gudonuv* together, we drove to Cork airport and I put him on a plane home. Naturally I took possession of the machine. The dial was rusty and stuck on PEEZINGDON, but I sprayed WD40 on it and immediately summoned blizzards and hail in the back garden for twenty minutes. (Apologies to people in the Timoleague area for last week when I made it rain garden furniture for a couple of hours. I was just getting my hand in.) I actually plan to use the machine – once I've understood it properly, to turn West Cork into a sunny Riviera where it only rains at night, if at all. I'm going to call my enterprise West Cork Sunny Weather Station. Though it might be strenuous work, turning the dial round from *sunny* to *very sunny* every day, business projections suggest I could make a modest living by charging a nominal public subscription for keeping the weather set fair. So I'm asking the people of West Cork to send donations to my hot weather operation fund of fifty euro a month each – because I'm not greedy. All contributions in brown envelopes. Addressed to I.Wild. C/O *Starlife* magazine. We'll all agree I know, fifty euro a month is cheap at the price. Otherwise, I'm afraid I'll have to leave ye singing in the rain. And after another summer like the last one, I'm pretty certain it'll be in gloomy operatic Russian.

Halloween special

This week I was invited to the first Hag of Beara Weekend, two days of workshops celebrating the magic of the Beara peninsula and beyond. Set in a desolate mountain landscape, with black bunting fluttering over a scaffolding stage, the festival attracted plenty of visitors. Many families came for a day out, and gathered round stalls to sample moth and pumpkin soup ladled from a bubbling cauldron or the delicious crusty bat pies. In marquees dotted around the site there were seminars on herbal remedies, cursing for beginners, and homework-writing spells for the kids. At one stall a woman with long silver hair stood behind piles of a self-published book entitled: *If You Don't Buy This, You'll Suffer Misfortune,* which was selling like Harry Potter. As with many festivals the weekend had been plagued by terrible weather – bright sunshine had ruined innumerable events.

I'd arrived to witness a festival highlight: the International Miss Witch Competition. Unfortunately, due to a demonstration spell-casting duel (which I'd missed), the person I was supposed to be interviewing had been turned into a newt. I eventually found Wanda Swish, the organiser of the event, in a ditch of brown water behind the sponsor's tent. After much coaxing, and with Wanda insisting the other witch had cheated, she agreed to clamber up my leg and onto my shoulder for a chat.

"Now Wanda," I asked the newt, as we browsed the stalls, "about the Miss Witch Competition – is it a sort of alternative Rose of Tralee?"

"No," she squeaked, "this is the finals of an international contest open to weird sisters of all nations. Ireland hasn't previously had a venue to stage the event.

It's more like a supernatural Miss World. Our entry's standing over there in the black robes…"

I was directed towards an unlovely young crone by the name of Miss Hildegard O'Rourke. Wanda introduced me and I asked Hildegard what it meant to be taking part in the finals. She cackled loudly.

"Oh it's a tremendous feeling to get up there in a bikini to show off my warts and misshapen body."

Wanda piped up to say that judges in the regional finals had been very impressed with Hildegard's hook nose, black teeth and deep wrinkles. They were certainly startling for a 21-year-old. Uncertain if they were the result of stage make-up I asked:

"Are they all yours?"

Hildegard screeched:

"*Course they are*! You don't get a conk like this unless witchcraft has run in your family for generations! I don't agree with plastic surgery or putting an eagle's beak on your nose and saying a spell to get the two to blend together. I'm all witch. Put me in a ducking stool and I'll float."

At this point, in trying to whisper at my ear, Wanda fell down the collar of my shirt and went wriggling down my back in that cold clammy way newts have. I collapsed in a fit of ticklish giggles and it was some minutes before order was restored.

"I was trying to tell you that Hilda's sackcloth bikini has been universally admired." Wanda squeaked once she was reinstated on my shoulder.

Hildegard smiled blackly, and for a terrifying moment I thought she was going to disrobe and give us a twirl.

"I think people want their witches disgusting don't you?" she croaked. "None of this Sabrina-type, long-haired beauty in a moon and stars swimming costume. That's a travesty of everything a real witch stands for. Makes me want to push 'em off their broomstick in mid-air it does." Hildegard gave a wrinkly scowl: "Or curse them. I've turned quite a few into newts like Wanda over the years. And Judges too, for giving me second or third place."

I was a little shocked by this.

"Isn't that cheating?"

"Fair is foul and foul is fair." Wanda and Hildegard intoned together.

At which point there was a loud crackle of thunder and a sudden downpour of rain. Delighted cries arose from around the festival site.

"Oh good." Wanda cried clapping her webbed hands together, "The thunder's come out."

"I'd better be off." Hildegard cackled, "The girls are lining up in their bikinis."

I wished her luck with winning Miss Witch 2011.

"Well, it really gets down to who the judges are most scared of. I've met the Miss English Witch and she looks a nasty piece of work. Some of the Eastern European girls look like they eat a Hansel and Gretel every morning for breakfast. We'll just have to see who's still standing when the hurly-burly's done."

As it looked like she was going to remove the robe any moment, I hastened away explaining that Wanda needed returning to her ditch. Unfortunately, I tripped over a large pile of books entitled: *If You Don't Buy This You'll Suffer Misfortune,* and Wanda went flying into a bowl of pumpkin broth. Several bystanders were scalded by splashes of hot soup and came after me shouting incantations. I only escaped by snatching somebody's broomstick and taking off up into the storm. But ... one story at a time.

WE HAVE THE TECHNOLOGY

There's a reason sport and politics shouldn't mix. Take the Rugby World Cup for instance. It seems that by loafing in front of a plasma TV to watch thirty incredible hulks wrestle what looks like an alien's head over a white line, I'm able to conveniently forget about innumerable worrying events cropping up all over the globe. Amazing! In fact, by navigating a path through various sporting tournaments throughout the year, it's almost possible for me to blank out that some people still believe in stoning and nuclear power. My guess is that if ornithologists actually peered into an ostrich's hole in the ground, they'd find a tiny plasma TV showing avian Olympics on Sky.

Anyhow, there I was a few days ago, head stuck in the sands of sport, cheering a try and forgetting entirely about the March of Regress, when a slow-motion camera showed that I'd been cheering a referee's mistake. The player had slid into touch just before the ball crossed the line and the ref didn't call for a review when he should have.

"Christ," some feller says beside me, "we have the technology, use it!"

At which point, inexplicably, sport and politics mixed in my mind. Even before a conversion sailed between the giant H of the posts, I realised we could eradicate the world's problems by applying technology to politics and in particular – *politicians.* And we wouldn't need to watch rugby ever again.

Now I sense here, heads of state spluttering in rage: President Sarkozy choking on his croissant as he reads this column in the Élysèe Palace ... Putin in the Kremlin giving his *Southern Star* a contemptuous smack of the hand ...Interpreters in Beijing trying desperately to calm Hu

Jintao as, having got through the Clonakilty notes, they read these words aloud to the communist central committee.

"Why apply technology to us?" I hear them wail in a rake of languages: "Tis not our fault that people believe in stoning and nuclear power."

But my point is this: these folk with the combed hair and fine dentistry get up on their soapboxes at election time promising us the moon and stars if we tighten the stringy belts on our trousers and then ten years later nothing's been done. In fact, things have only got worse. Don't tell me it's all down to the intractable nature of the planet's predicament – a dearth of probity in politicians has blighted civilisation since the Ancient Greeks first cast a vote. The fact is, the kind of people who shin to the top of the greasy pole in search of power are often interested in nothing more than telling us one thing and doing another. Often as not they tell us the very opposite of what they know to be true. By the time we kick them out, the earth's problems have snowballed.

Which brings me back to the rugby. Now I'm not suggesting we send out national politicians fifteen a side and watch them scrummage and maul across a rugby pitch as an answer to our social and economic problems. However symbolically apt it might seem to have opposing parties wrestling in the mud and kicking each other in the teeth, and however diverting as a spectacle, (let's be honest, it would be more absorbing to watch than any current political programme and you might find out who was *really* up to putting in 80 minutes for their country) it wouldn't stop rainforests being felled. No, I'm talking about the way that rugby uses cutting-edge technology to establish the truth of whether the alien's head actually went over the line. In the past, we only had the ref's word for it. Now, we can go over it frame by frame in slow motion from any number of angles and get a pretty good approximation of the truth.

Why not do the same with our politicians? Where would the difficulty be in say, strapping lie detectors to those who hold high office? These contraptions needn't be huge. Nowadays they can be micro devices no bigger than a tiepin. Politicians would be required to wear a fib detector at all times – it could even be implanted under the skin. A noisy alarm would be set off whenever the politician told a whopper. One can imagine transcriptions from Hansard in the UK:

"My Right Honourable Gentlemen, beep beeeeeep beeeep".

"On the contrary, if the Right Honourable beeeep beep."

I know your Sarkozys and Putins and Jintaos might find all manner of excuses for refusing to wear the contraption. But surely it's the same argument that they always give with regard to street surveillance cameras in cities. As they say, if you've nothing to hide, why would it bother you?

The advantages for us all are obvious. A question that might have been put to President Bush such as, "Are prisoners being tortured in Guantanamo Bay?" would be answered "No. Beeep beeeeeeep beeeeeep!"

Or perhaps, aware that we could see their noses growing, our political Pinocchios would never transgress in the first place. They might start acting on world problems instead of filling fertilizer sacks with cash confetti. All I'm saying is, the technology is there. We should use it.

About the Author

Ian Wild is a writer and theatre composer from Enniskean, Co. Cork. He has won numerous writing awards, including *The Aeon Short Story Prize* 2012 and the *Fish International Short Story Prize* 2009. Four of his highly successful musical comedies appeared in Cork Midsummer Festivals: *The Pirates in Short Pants, Marco Polo's Toilet Brush, Rachmaninov's Maid* and *Spaghetti Western.* His broadcast work includes *Way Out West* – a comedy series for RTE Radio One; and over twenty children's stories for RTE's *Fiction Fifteen.* His play Mrs Shakespeare won the Argus Fringe Theatre award in 2015.

34707072R00066

Printed in Poland
by Amazon Fulfillment
Poland Sp. z o.o., Wrocław